Mem Fox
pictures by David Miller

PUFFIN BOOKS

I'd dance with a
pig
in a shiny green
wig

But I wouldn't say

"BOO!"

to a goose.

I'd ride on a 'roo
to Kalamazoo

But I wouldn't say "BOO!" to a goose.

I'd dive from a
mountain
right into a
fountain

But I wouldn't say

"BOO!"

to a goose.

I'd play with a snake

if I found one **awake**

But I wouldn't say

"*BOO!*"

to a goose.

I'd gobble up
snails
from smelly old
pails

But I wouldn't say "BOO!" to a goose.

I'd take a long
walk
from here to
New York

But I wouldn't say

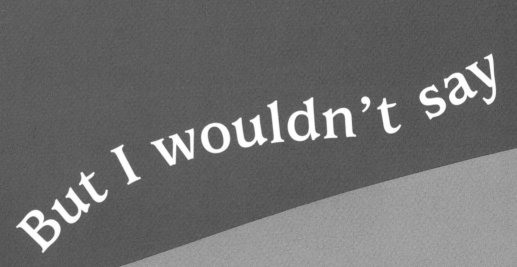

"BOO!" to a goose.

I'd swim with a
whale
without going
pale

But I wouldn't say "BOO!" to a goose.

I'd feed my pajamas

I'd walk down the
street
with balloons on my
feet

I'd dye my hair **yellow**
and make Grandma
bellow

But I wouldn't say

"BOO!" to a goose.

I'd walk on my
knees
past a hive full of
bees

But I wouldn't say "BOO!" to a goose.

I'd eat all the **butter** from here to Calcutta

I'd skip across **town**
with my pants hanging
down

But I wouldn't say

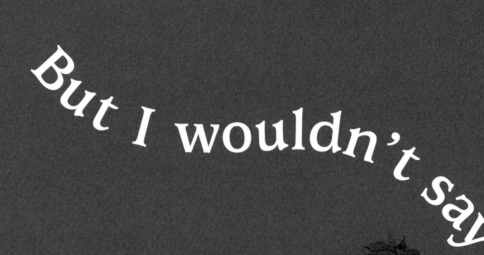

"BOO!"

to a goose.

I'd do all these
things quite
bravely – you'd see!

But I wouldn't say
"BOO!"
to one goose or three

because...

a goose once said

"BOO!"

to me!

FOR JÜRGEN, AT LAST
M.F.

FOR SYLVIA
D.M.

PUFFIN BOOKS
Published by the Penguin Group
Penguin Putnam Books for Young Readers, 345 Hudson Street, New York, New York 10014, U.S.A.
Penguin Books Ltd., 27 Wrights Lane, London W8 5TZ, England
Penguin Books Australia Ltd., Ringwood, Victoria, Australia
Penguin Books Canada Ltd., 10 Alcorn Avenue, Toronto, Ontario, Canada M4V 3B2
Penguin Books (N.Z.) Ltd., 182-190 Wairau Road, Auckland 10, New Zealand

Penguin Books Ltd., Registered Offices: Harmondsworth, Middlesex, England

Published in Australia and New Zealand by Hachette Children's Books Australia,
an imprint of Hachette Lirve Australia Pty Limited,
First published in the United States of America by Dial Books for Young Readers,
a division of Penguin Books USA Inc., 1998
Published by Puffin Books, a division of Penguin Putnam Books for Young Readers, 2001

5 7 9 10 8 6 4

Text copyright © Mem Fox, 1996
Illustrations copyright © David Miller, 1996
All rights reserved

THE LIBRARY OF CONGRESS HAS CATALOGED THE DIAL EDITION AS FOLLOWS:
Fox, Mem, date.
Boo to a Goose/Mem Fox; pictures by David Miller.—1st ed.   p.   cm.
Summary: A boy relates a long list of things he would do before he'd say boo to a goose.
ISBN 0-8037-2274-5
[1. Geese—Fiction. 2. Stories in rhyme. 3. Humorous stories.]
I. Miller, David, date, ill. II. Title. PZ8.3.F8245Bo 1998 [E]—dc21 96-54225 CIP AC

Puffin Books ISBN 0-14-056766-6
Printed in China

The art for this book was created with paper sculpture.